Bi... 04.

go Sailing

☆ Selina Young ☆

Blue Bananas

First published in Great Britain 2000
This edition published 2002
by Egmont Books Limited
239 Kensington High Street, London W8 6SA
Published in hardback by Heinemann Library,
a division of Reed Educational and Professional Printing Ltd
by arrangement with Egmont Books Limited
Text and illustrations copyright © Selina Young 2000
The author and the illustrator have asserted their moral rights
Paperback ISBN 1 4052 0256 4
Hardback ISBN 0 431 06984 0
10 9 8 7 6 5 4 3 2
A CIP catalogue record for this title
is available from the British Library
Printed and bound in the U.A.E

Big Dog was an inventor.
Some days he invented lots of things
and some days he didn't.

Last Tuesday Little Dog helped
Big Dog make a shiny red boat.
(Just like that!)

Big dog bounced out of bed extra early

and bounded noisily down the stairs.

Little Dog was still snuggled up in bed when Big Dog burst in with the breakfast tray.

6

Big Dog ate his breakfast and talked excitedly with his mouth full. Today was the day for trying out their new boat.

Little Dog thought this sounded fun
so she got up and washed behind her
ears and put on a clean scarf.

Big Dog made a list of all the things

they should take with them.

Little Dog packed all the things into
a big basket. She put in her umbrella
just in case.

Big Dog made his favourite sandwiches,

peanut butter, cheese and jam.

At last they were ready to go.

Big Dog was so excited he raced

out of the door and ran on ahead.

The boat was tied to the jetty.

It bobbed up and down in the water.

Big Dog galloped up the gangplank
and leapt on board.

Big Dog and Little Dog's boat
was made out of lots of
bits and bobs. It had:

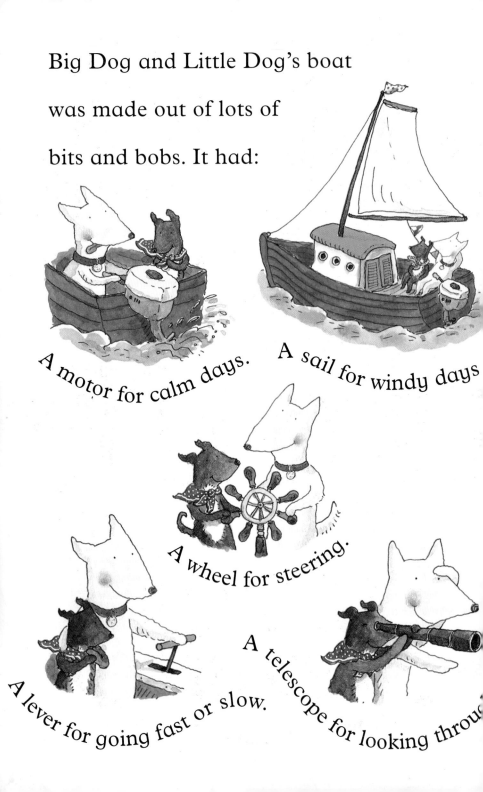

A motor for calm days.

A sail for windy days

A wheel for steering.

A lever for going fast or slow.

A telescope for looking throu

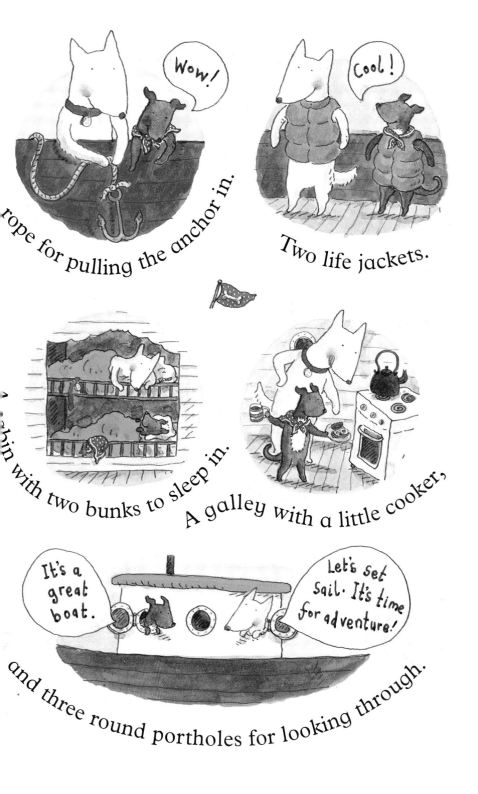

rope for pulling the anchor in.

Two life jackets.

...bin with two bunks to sleep in.

A galley with a little cooker,

and three round portholes for looking through.

Big Dog turned the key and the engine started. Chug splutter chug chug. Carefully he steered the boat through the harbour and out to sea.

Then Big Dog pushed the lever to 'Fast'
and off they zoomed. Their ears flapped
as they whizzed along. The boat went
thump thump against the waves.

Big Dog thought that going fast was amazing. Little Dog wasn't so sure. She'd rather be fishing.

Big Dog stopped the boat in a shady

cove and dropped the anchor with a

S P L O S H!

They got out their fishing rods and
Big Dog helped Little Dog put bait
on her hook.

Big Dog and Little Dog threw their
lines out to sea and waited for the fish
to start biting.

It wasn't long before Big Dog felt

a sharp tug. It must be a fish!

He pulled on his line.

It was hard work.

A horrible monster with spikes

came flying out of the water.

The spiky fish pulled itself free and swam away.

'I don't like fishing any more,' said Big Dog. 'Let's do something more exciting.'

'Like what?' asked Little Dog.

After that they went snorkelling.

Big Dog took a bag to collect shells.

One, two, three, they jumped into the

water with a big splash.

Snorkelling was fun.

Little Dog liked counting the fish.

Big Dog was busy seeing how many

shells he could fit in his bag.

When Big Dog's bag was full of shells,
they swam back to the boat for some
lunch.

After lunch the sky got darker and a terrible storm began to blow. Big Dog and Little Dog went down below to make some hot chocolate, and warm up.

Big Dog was just pouring the milk into the mugs when **Bump!** the boat hit something!

They'd crashed into a big island.

Big Dog dropped the anchor and

Little Dog lowered the gangplank.

Little Dog fetched her umbrella and

Big Dog grabbed his telescope. Then

they ran ashore.

'Let's explore,' said Big Dog. Together they ran up the hill to the top of the island. It was very hard work. The ground was so shiny and slippery.

I can feel rain drops.

At the top of the island they sat down and took turns to look through the telescope.

Then Big Dog felt rain drops.

Plip plop! Big drops of rain began to fall out of the sky. But there was not a rain cloud in sight. Little Dog put up her umbrella. Splish splash went the rain.

Suddenly there was a big rumble and the island began to shake. It was so bumpy Big Dog and Little Dog fell over and tumbled down the hill.

They jumped aboard their boat and hid
under their bunks.

Just then a big voice said, 'Whoops!
I've bumped into someone's boat.
I hope I didn't tip them out.'

Little Dog peeped out from under the
table and saw a big black eye at the
porthole. A deep voice said: 'Hello,
anyone at home?'

Big Dog and Little Dog came out from their hiding places but all they could see was the island.

'I'm sorry I bumped you,' the voice continued kindly. 'I always seem to be bumping into something. Last week it was the lighthouse and it hurt my nose.'

The whale explained how he kept
falling asleep and drifting into things.
He showed Big Dog and Little Dog all
his bumps and bruises.(They were very
sympathetic.)

Little Dog suddenly had an idea.

She whispered into Big Dog's ear.

'Good thinking!' said Big Dog. 'Whale

can have our anchor!'

The whale thought it was such a brilliant idea he offered Big Dog and Little Dog a ride home on his back.

What an exciting boat adventure they'd
had. Little Dog helped Big Dog pull the
boat up on the beach. Then they raced
home for tea.

Big Dog cooked some fish fingers.

Little Dog mashed some potatoes.

Then it was time for bed.

Little Dog went to sleep straight away.

But Big Dog was wide awake planning

a very special outing for next weekend.